I USED TO BE AN ARTICHOKE

I USED TO BE AN ARTICHOKE

written by Maureen McGinn
art by Anita Norman

CONCORDIA
Publishing House
St. Louis London

This book is dedicated to
Dr. Dick Miller, The B.F.A.A.,
and to my comfortably—
lovely family.

Concordia Publishing House, St. Louis, Missouri
Concordia Publishing House Ltd., London E. C. 1
Copyright © 1973 Concordia Publishing House
International Standard Book No. 0-570-03421-3
MANUFACTURED IN THE UNITED STATES OF AMERICA

I used to be an ARTICHOKE . . .

But one day someone passed me by
And said, "What an *ugly* ARTICHOKE!"
So I became a . . .

BUTTERFLY.

I was a beautiful BUTTERFLY,
But my colors would not stay on.
They always washed off in the rain,
So, I changed into a . . .

CRAYON.

I was a lovely purple CRAYON,
But I felt like I was *dyin'*
When I was left out in the sun,
So, I became a . . .

DANDELION.

I was minding my own business,
When a man began to beg,
"Please go away, Mr. DANDELION."
So, I changed into an . . .

EGG.

Not an ordinary EGG, a snake EGG!
And I woke up beneath a log.
I said, "Oh no, this ain't for me!"
And I changed into a . . .

FROG.

I was happy as a FROG,
Sitting all day in the sun.
But someone said they'd *eat* my legs,
So I became a . . .

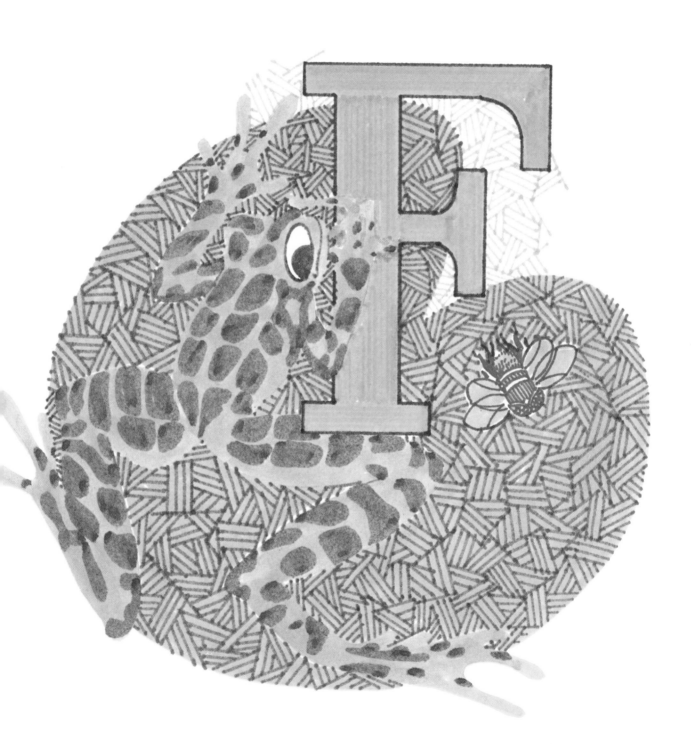

GUN,

A bright red, plastic WATERGUN,
And I stayed that way until
Once at school I was used on a teacher,
Then I changed into a . . .

HILL.

I certainly wasn't very big,
But I thought, "Being small is nice"
(Till they leveled me for a highway).
Then I changed into some . . .

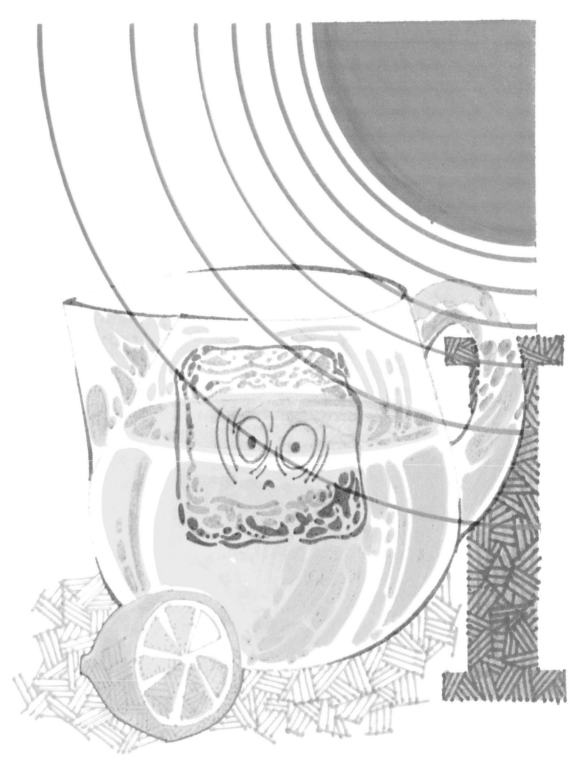

ICE.

I was swimming in some lemonade
At a lemonade stand and
Just before I started to melt,
I became a jar of . . .

JAM.

Now, JAM is fine just by itself,
But peanut butter will *never* do.
We always seemed to be together,
So I changed into a . . .

KANGAROO.

I lived in Australia
And that didn't matter,
But I got homesick after a while
And changed into a . . .

LADDER.

Little did I know that being
A LADDER isn't funny.
I discovered I was afraid of heights
And changed into some . . .

MONEY.

I lived with lots of other MONEY
In the biggest bank you've ever seen.
But one day when the bank got robbed,
I became a . . .

NECTARINE.

NECTARINEs are thin-skinned,
And I really couldn't see a
***Future* in a NECTARINE.**
So, I became an . . .

ONOMATOPOEIA.

I always said just what I meant;
I was honest as I could be.
But "ONOMATOPOEIA" is hard to spell,
So, I changed into a . . .

PEA.

I was happy living in my pod,
But the other PEAs were mean.
And so, unlike most podded PEAs,
I changed into a . . .

QUEEN.

Being a QUEEN was so much fun;
Upon my throne I sat,
Until I heard, "The land's at war!"
And I changed into a . . .

RAT.

But nobody really likes a RAT.
(You know how dirty they are.)
One day I said, "This is no way to live.
I think I'll be a . . .

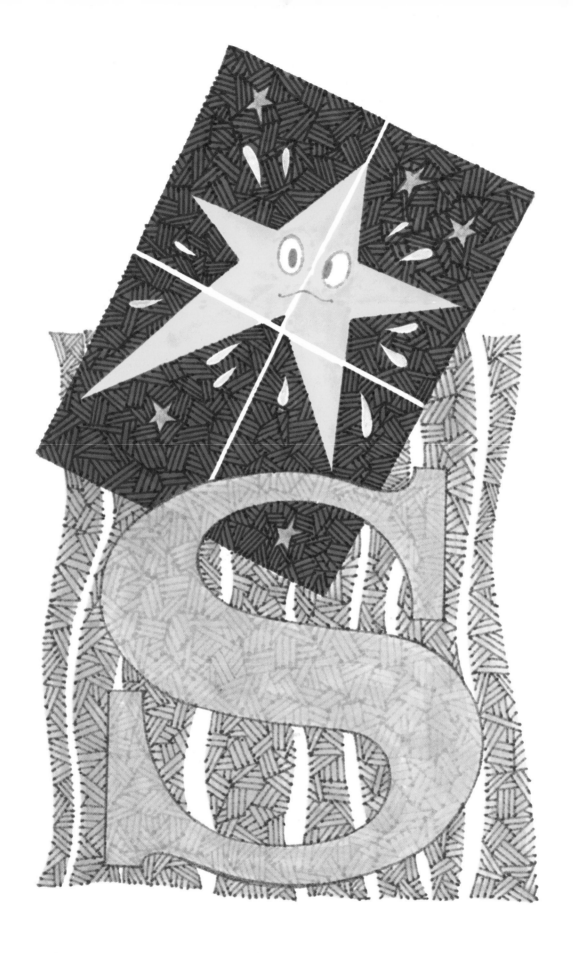

STAR."

After I was a STAR awhile,
I started to burn up.
And, wanting to get back to the earth,
I changed into a . . .

TURNIP.

But it was cold beneath the ground;
There wasn't any heat down there.
And I knew there was just one thing to do.
I did it. I became . . .

UNDERWEAR.

UNDERWEAR's fine in the winter,
But when it gets warm *I'll bet*
You'd rather be something else too.
I changed into a . . .

VIOLET.

**VIOLETs are pretty,
But VIOLETs are small.
I wanted to be noticed.
So, I became a . . .**

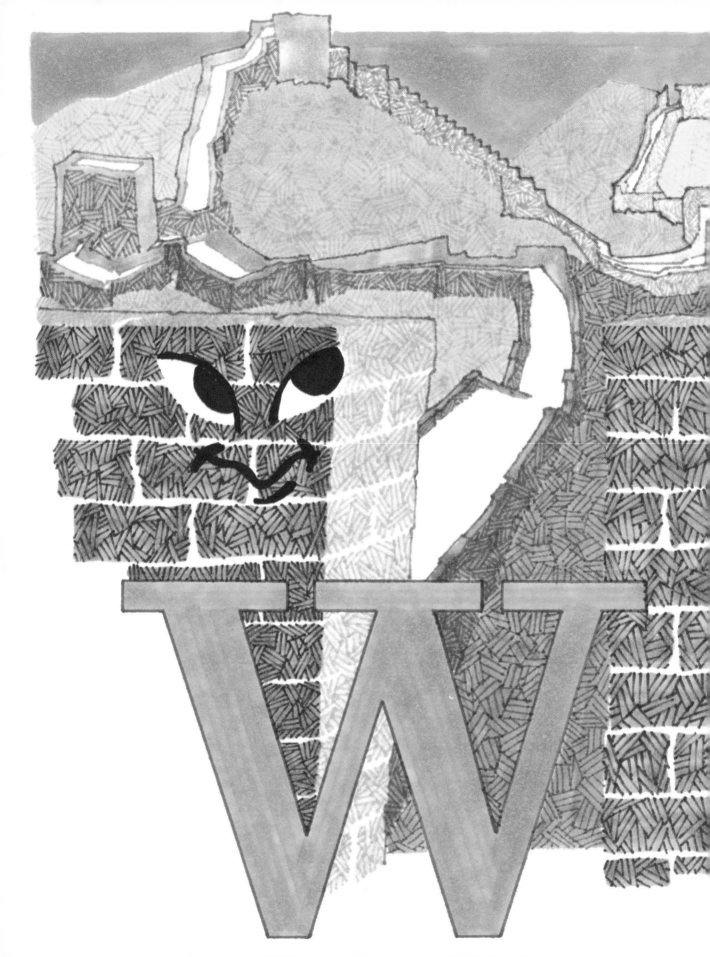

WALL.

I was the Great WALL of China,
The longest WALL you've ever seen.
But since WALLs often block the view,
I became an . . .

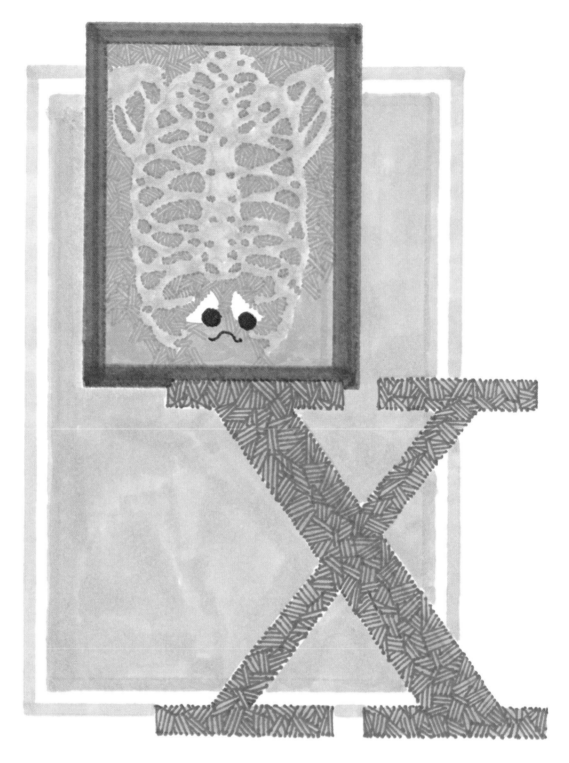

X-RAY MACHINE.

But X-RAYs live in hospitals;
They're not much fun, you know.
I wanted to have a good time,
So, I became a . . .

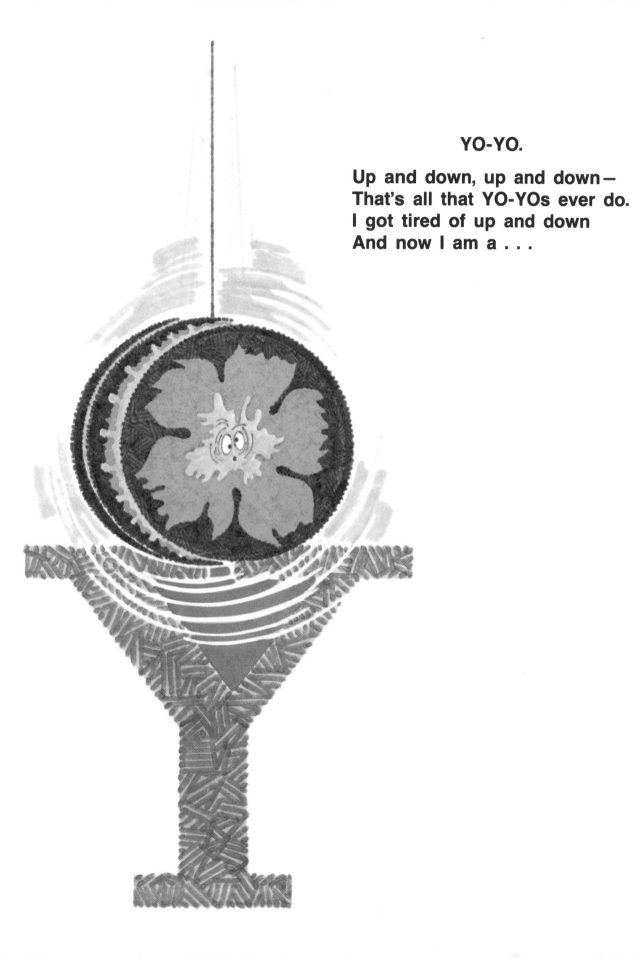

YO-YO.

Up and down, up and down—
That's all that YO-YOs ever do.
I got tired of up and down
And now I am a . . .

ZOO.

I suppose that you must envy me.

I've been things from A to Z.
I'll tell you something, and it's no joke . . .

I should have stayed an ARTICHOKE.